Snow White

and me!

For Hannah and Peter — E. B.

First published 2019 by Nosy Crow Ltd
The Crow's Nest, 14 Baden Place
Crosby Row, London SE1 1YW
www.nosycrow.com
ISBN 978 1 78800 302 5 (HB)
ISBN 978 1 78800 303 2 (PB)
Nosy Crow and associated logos are trademarks
and/or registered trademarks of Nosy Crow Ltd
Text © Nosy Crow Ltd 2019
Illustrations © Ed Bryan 2015
The right of Ed Bryan to be identified as the
illustrator of this work has been asserted.

A CIP catalogue record for this book is available from the British Library.
Printed in China
Papers used by Nosy Crow are made from wood grown in
sustainable forests.
1 3 5 7 9 8 6 4 2 (HB)
1 3 5 7 9 8 6 4 2 (PB)

Snow White

 nosy crow

Illustrated by
Ed Bryan

Once upon a time on a snowy winter's day, a **queen** was sewing in a room at the top of her castle when she pricked her finger.

"How I **wish** I had a daughter with lips as **red** as this blood, with skin as **white** as this snow and hair as **black** as these ebony window frames," she said.

The queen's wish came true, and soon her beautiful **baby girl** was born.

But the queen died soon after and her husband, the **king**, was left to bring up the princess on his own. He decided to call her **Snow White**.

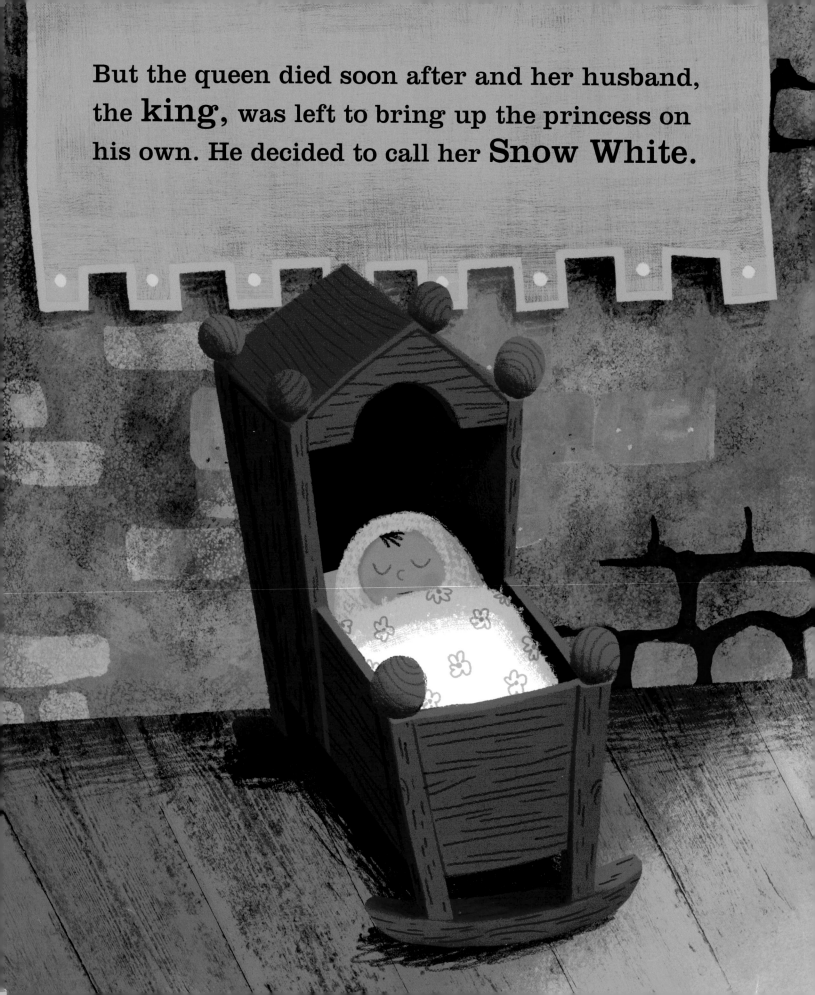

The king wasn't alone for long though.
He married again. His second wife was very
beautiful, but she was really a **cruel witch**.

She had a **magic mirror** and she always asked it the same question, "Magic mirror on the wall, who is the fairest of them all?"

And the mirror would reply,
"There is no doubt, my gracious queen,
you are the fairest ever seen."

The queen **hated** Snow White. She was jealous of how much the king loved her, and she made her work hard, **cleaning** the castle and **washing** clothes.

Snow White wished she could tell her father how **mean** her stepmother was to her, but she knew he would not listen.

Time passed and Snow White grew up. One day, when the queen asked her mirror who the most beautiful woman in the land was, the mirror had a **very different** reply . . .

"I'm magic so
I must speak true –
Snow White
is fairer, now,
than you."

"That silly girl?"
the wicked queen shrieked.
"You **can't** be serious!"

Later that day, the evil queen ordered the castle huntsman to **kill** Snow White . . .

. . . but the huntsman felt sorry for Snow White, so he took her into the forest and told her to **run away.**

All night long, Snow White
wandered through the deep, dark forest.

When the sun rose, she came across a strange little **house** in a clearing. She pushed open the door and walked inside . . .

The house was lovely but **very** messy, so she decided to tidy and clean.

What she didn't know was that the little house belonged to **seven dwarfs,** who spent their days deep underground, looking for jewels.

That evening, the seven dwarfs came home
to find their house **sparkling clean**,
with Snow White fast asleep at the table.

When she woke up, the
dwarfs listened to her story.

They were happy for her to come
and live in their house with them.

And they lived **very** happily, until . . .

. . . one day, the queen asked her mirror, "Magic mirror on the wall, who is the fairest of them all?"

The mirror replied, "Although she's **hidden** far from sight, the fairest woman is Snow White."

The wicked queen gave a cry. **"I've been tricked!"** she screamed. "I'll find Snow White and **kill** her myself!"

Using her magic, the queen **disguised** herself as an old woman. Then she cooked up a special **poison** and dipped an apple into it.

That afternoon, Snow White opened the door
to find an **old woman** standing there.

"Hello. I am a poor pedlar woman. Would you like
one of my **delicious** apples?" she said.

"Thank you. I **do** like apples," said Snow White.

But no sooner had
Snow White taken a bite
than she **fell** to the
floor in a **deep sleep**.

When the dwarfs got home, they found her lying as still as a statue.

Days passed and Snow White didn't wake up.
The dwarfs placed her in a special glass box in
the forest, and kept watch over her day and night.

One day, a **prince** walked by. He thought Snow White's face was so **kind** and **gentle** that he begged the dwarfs to help him move her to his palace.

The dwarfs picked up Snow White in her glass box, but it was **SO** heavy that it fell to the ground and . . .

CRASH! The box shattered!

The piece of poisoned apple popped out of Snow White's mouth and she woke up.

"Goodness! What happened?" said Snow White.

"You've been asleep for **ages**," said the dwarfs.
"But we're so happy you're awake!"

"It's a **pleasure** to meet you,
Snow White," said the prince.

When Snow White's father found out what the wicked queen had done, he **imprisoned** her in the tower . . .

. . . and Snow White and the dwarfs stayed at the prince's palace.

As the days went by,
the prince and Snow White
fell in **love** and were married.

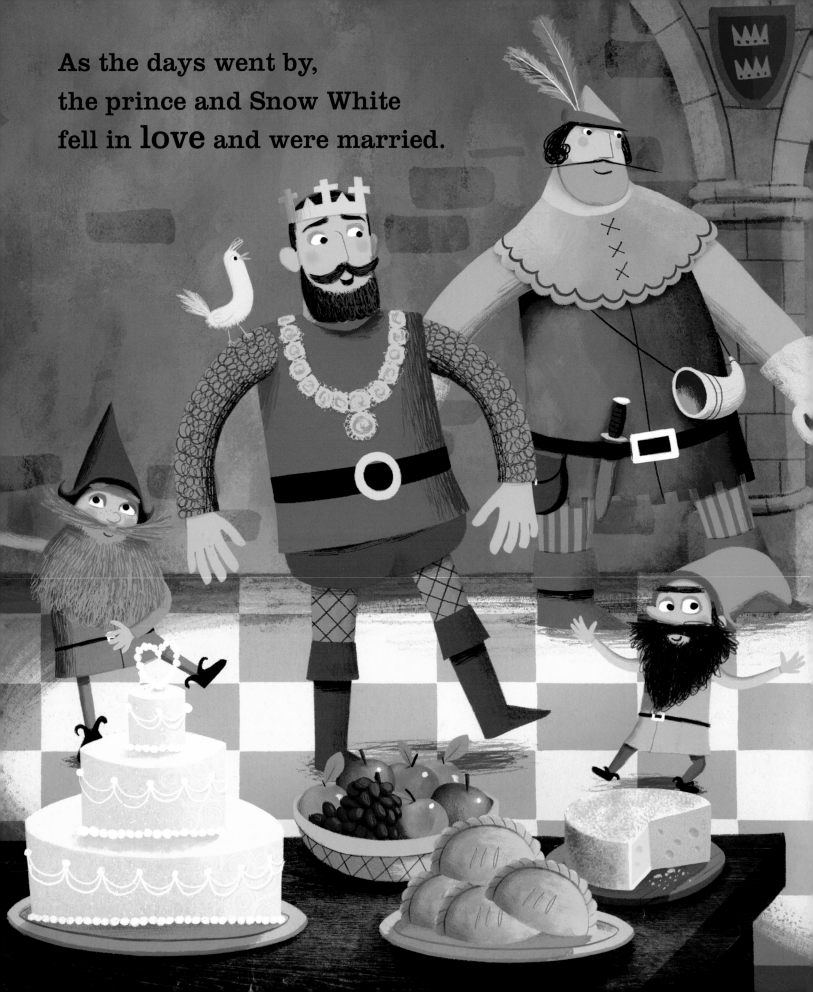

The guests danced **all night long . . .**

. . . and they all lived
happily ever after.

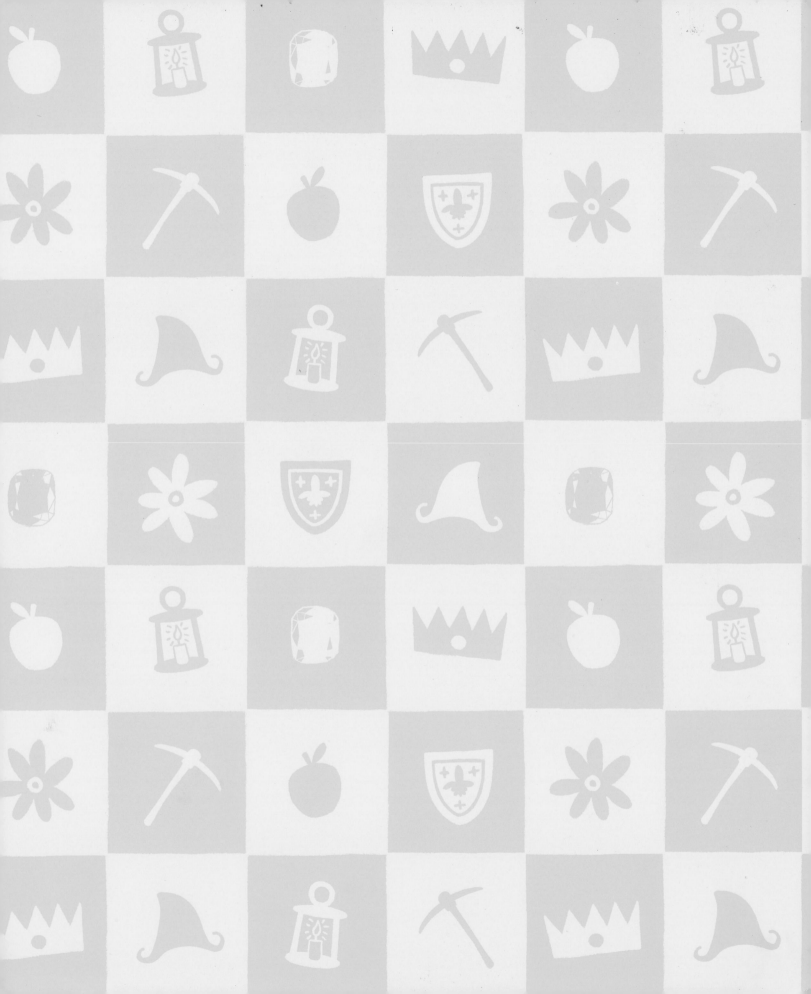

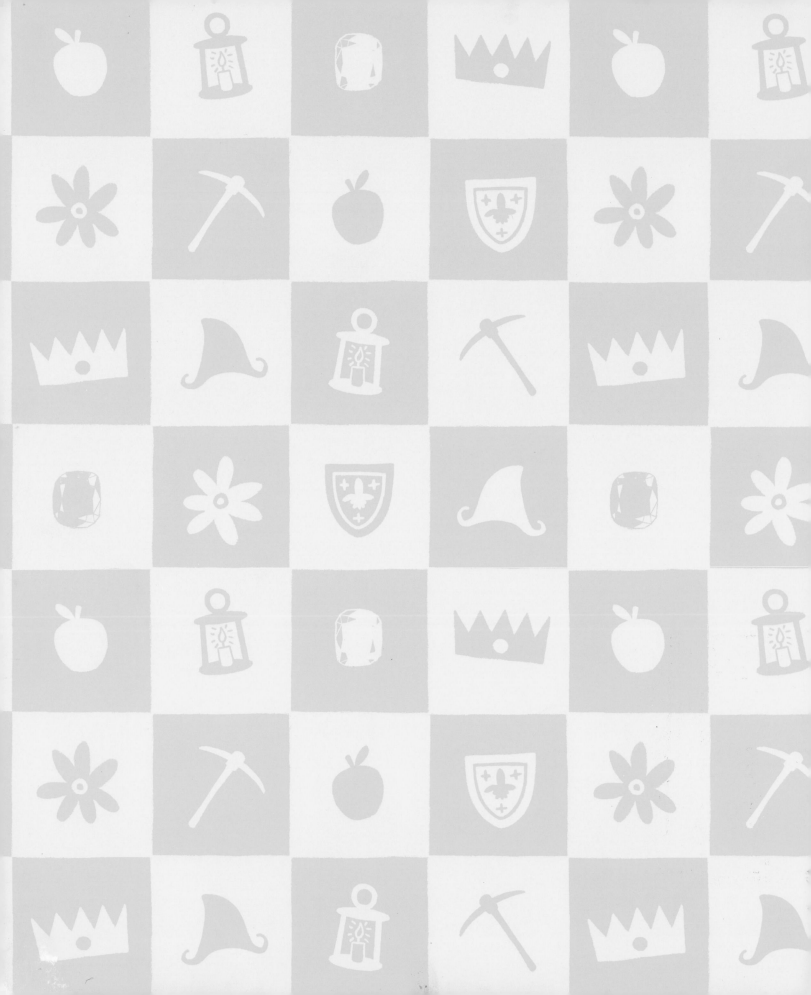